C000201181

The
Visitor

CHRIS SIMPSON

MᶜNIDDER | &
GRACE

The Visitor

CHRIS SIMPSON

Published by McNidder & Grace
Aswarby House
Aswarby
Lincolnshire NG34 8SE

www.mcnidderandgrace.co.uk

First published in The Netherlands, 2000

This new edition h/b published in the UK, 2017

A catalogue record for this work is available from
the British Library.

ISBN: 9780857161758

Cover illustration: courtesy of Terry Logan

Designed by Obsidian Design

Printed in the EU by Pulsio Ltd

DEDICATION

To the memory of George W. Smith, who died tragically on the 14 April 1911. He was a farmer and the grandfather I never knew and, to the very best of my knowledge, he was an essentially good man in all aspects of his life. He was the role model for the character of Jos Robertshaw in this story.

ABOUT THE AUTHOR

Chris Simpson began life in an old stone house on a hilltop in Nidderdale, without the luxury of electricity. He refers to it as a golden time. Educated at Harrogate Grammar School and King's College, London, his guitar took him on a journey across the world. He has written some twenty-five albums for his band, Magna Carta, toured seventy-eight countries across forty-eight years and sold eight million records. The Dales background left an indelible mark on his writing. For much of his time, he lives with his wife Cathy on a Narrowboat, near Skipton, North Yorkshire.

ACKNOWLEDGMENTS

So many grateful thanks are owed. To my gorgeous wife, Cathy, ever a great love and companion, whose capacity to put up with the author's 'little moments' borders on the miraculous. To the late Frank and Mary Simpson, without whom there would be no Visitor. To Spencer Leigh for opening the door to the publishing house McNidder & Grace; to the painstaking Andy Peden Smith, publisher extraordinaire and the people of Nidderdale and Wharfedale who unwittingly lent so much colour to this story. Kate Smith, farmer of Ripley, whose late mother's legendary farmhouse table at Christmas is reproduced here unabridged. Laurie the postman, Andrew Jackson the Doctor and the many Walters and Jos Robertshaws I chanced to meet along the way, all adding to the richness: such timeless characters who enriched the potpourri of Dales life, and to whom I am deeply grateful.

They are the bastions of a sadly vanishing world.

Chapter 1

SUNDAY, 22 DECEMBER: EVENING

THE NORTH wind had come far.

A restless traveller, he never paused even for a moment and his icy breath, born in the jutted ice and frozen deserts of the Arctic, withered all it touched as it dusted the land with dry powdery snow.

Above, in the great arch of the sky, the stars winked and flashed between ramparts of cloud, while across the hill country below an awed hush hung suspended in time between keening gusts of wind. In the breaks of pine that dotted the fellsides, the sound was akin to the scend of the sea upon some forgotten shore.

Here and there among the wild landscape,

solitary lights, like pin holes through the blanket of the dark, shone brave and tiny in the black winter night.

It was Christmas time and for every light there was a little world of warmth and bustle, of steaming kitchens and clattering farm machinery. Each was an island, a refuge from the iron fist of winter that could so easily crush everything in its path.

Far away, on either side of the hill country, to the east and the west, the glow of the great cities paled the sky. It was a different world, albeit with the same purpose: to prepare for and celebrate Christmas.

This was a world of clamour and dazzling lights, of crowded pavements and human rivers about to burst their banks and overflow on to the roads. To untutored ears, unaccustomed to the ways and sounds of the city, it was a bewildering cacophony of voices and car engines, myriad footsteps and the incessant tinkling of cash registers in the overheated department stores, of music, loud and raucous, pumped from the doorways of the brightly lit boutiques and the endless bars advertising "festive" discounts and jammed to bursting one minute and spilling their cheerful clientele back out onto the street the next. All was hurry and excess, with year-long caution dissipated in a lemming-like rush to spend.

***

Far away from the cities, the halo of man-made lights dwindled to nothing and the power of the heavens took over again. The wind twisted and turned between the flanks of the hills and whirled spinning columns of snowflakes across a cobbled street.

It was a simple north country village. The houses were of stone, built to stand against the weather, and across the square the coloured lights tapped against the shop windows as the Christmas tree swayed in the wind.

It was quieter here, much quieter than the city. The imposing mass of the uplands flanked the village on all sides like great unmoving whales, their tops dusted with snow, spectral white in the occasional glimpses of moonlight between the driving squalls.

One main road linked the village to the market town a dozen miles away. Another led upwards, connecting the villages at the head of the dale where it wound in a series of hairpin bends up and over the summit, to descend into the valley beyond.

There was one other road that climbed steeply up into the hills on the northeast side. It was as if the original road builders of long ago had run out of inspiration, for the tarmac ended among the decaying workings of old lead mines and only a rough road carried on, bestrewn with ruts and potholes. Even that primitive highway finished abruptly where the moorland began.

Where the road ended there was a platform for milk churns and a gate in the wall over the cattle grid bearing a wooden sign with the faded legend "Keld House Farm". Beyond, a twin-track gravel road wound downwards to disappear around the contours of the land towards the Ghyll.

In the primeval darkness the welcoming lights of a farmhouse, nestling like a mother hen among its buildings, were the only signs of life in the bleak landscape. Here the force of the wind was broken by the hills and, ebbing and flowing in the night air, came the sound of the beck, tumbling between the boulders on its rocky course down the valley.

The house was a "long house", built in the style of the ancient Norsemen who bestowed the name "dalen" on this landscape, reminiscent of the lands they had left across the North Sea. Double-storeyed and roofed with great stone tiles, its mullioned windows glowed with curtained light. The barn and mistel were also part of the house, because, with the insight born of centuries of experience, the original builders knew that the warmth from the animals gave added heat. And when the snow was deep or storms raged over the land, they could still reach their beasts.

Overall, the heady scent of wood smoke mixed with the pungent aroma of a working farm.

Apart from the barn and mistel and big winter cattle shed, the outbuildings clustered about the farmhouse in no apparent order. An ancient tractor, rusty harrows and assorted machinery and straw bales filled one; scattered logs piled around a saw bench another and, beyond the pigsties, the terraced garden, walled to keep out the rabbits, sloped down to the tumbling beck.

The orchard lay to the south side of the house, raspberry canes around the perimeter. Plum, apple and pear trees, now crusted with snow, their sinews gnarled and twisted like old men, stooped away from the prevailing wind. A cobbled yard of old river stones lay before the house, warped and polished with time. Sheep pens stood on the one side, tool stores and yet more outhouses on the other.

The sheep dogs, Tip and Bess, were apparently oblivious to the weather, and lived in two barrels beneath the rusty old diesel tank. Chained at night, they were still within snapping reach of anyone who came to the door. By day they ranged far and wide, mudsplashed and sleek-bellied, close to the ground, working as one with the old man, reading his commands and anticipating the manoeuvrings of the sheep.

A narrow porch kept the wind from the kitchen door – the front door was never used

– its roof consisting of two great stone slabs rooted in the fabric of the building. A lucky horseshoe hung from a peg at the apex together with snares, weathering before use, and the worn, carved stone that bore the date, 1612.

Within the porch itself, smelling strongly of midden and cowshed, were several pairs of rubber boots, a shepherd's crook, a hurricane lantern on a hook and the old man's faded Barbour, draped carelessly from the haft of a yard broom.

***

Jos Robertshaw sat, legs outstretched, before the fire in the living room. The floors were stone-flagged with a rag rug before the old range, where a kettle whispered listlessly on the hob.

Above his head, the great beams supported the floor above. They were of seasoned oak and hard as steel, with strangely assorted cuts and grooves that bore no resemblance to the joists they supported, suggesting their probable origins as ships' timbers.

7

In the corner by the stairs a grandfather clock ticked sonorously, unhurriedly, as if each stroke of the pendulum might be its last, measuring the onward passage of time with ringing chimes upon the hour, the echoes of which still seemed to linger in the nooks and crannies of the room.

Against the opposite wall, a Welsh dresser supported a mixture of Delft pottery, pewter plates, cricket cups and sepia photographs of relatives and prize-winning animals. The television sat on a squat-legged table in a corner to be viewed on occasion but never turned on without good cause.

In the centre of the room stood a long, scrubbed pine table, knotted and scarred with the passage of years and laden with jars of pickles, mustard, a Christmas cake baked the year before and fortified with brandy, various cheeses, a cold joint of beef, a goose ready for stuffing, trays of sausage meat, mince pies, a large pork pie, a bottle of sherry, one of whisky and a deceptively potent home-made elderberry wine.

Hospitality was a matter of pride with the

hill farmer and, from the postman to the vicar, anyone coming over the threshold was assured of a dram or a drop of home-brewed beer, known affectionately as "lotion" and arguably more lethal than the dram.

Jos removed his glasses, pausing to wipe each lens with the slow deliberation that came from years of thinking carefully about anything before it was done. He came from a long line of Robertshaws who, as far as anyone could tell, had lived there since the living rock was quarried to build the house and the now great sycamores had been planted as saplings at the "weather end" to absorb the force of the gales. Different days, he mused, but none the worse for that, when a man toiled from dawn to dusk often for small returns, but in close harmony with the seasons.

He was, sadly, the last of his line to run "Keld" as a working farm. The big men far away in Brussels were making sure of that, with policies he hardly understood or could do nothing to prevent, slowly but surely throttling the life out of the hill farmer, with no regard for heritage or tradition. He was weary of the continual reminders of a changing world and the rush to be new and improved. Even Arnold, his only son, had seen no future in endless toil for no visible return and had headed for the city.

Jos put down the unread *Yorkshire Post* and once again picked up the letter.

'It's no use worriting Jos. We've agreed. He's coming and that's all there is to it.'

Emily sat in the chair opposite him, as ever, a rug over her thin frame, the grey eyes missing little. It cut him to the heart to see her like this, his rock and strength for so long, slipping slowly but surely away from him, prey to an illness now so common but bit by bit spreading its cruel fingers through her frail body. It had been some time ago that the pains had started and then the slow slide down into the weight loss and the frailty that soon accompanied the onward spread of the disease. In times gone by she was usually up before the sun – his "second good right arm", as he always called her – baking, washing, cooking, and making butter.

The tasks followed the round of the seasons; haymaking, lambing and clipping, birthing livestock, bottling and pickling were all part of the routine to Emily. That was until she was confined to the world of her chair. Now, he carried her to bed at night and Laura, the wife of Walter, his farm man, came in to clean and take care of baking and provisions.

Jos weighed his answer with care. 'Aye, but don't you think we've enough on what with Arnold and his, what do you call it, partner, coming Christmas Day?' He could not for the life of him understand where it was all going. In his day, marriage was marriage and mostly for life. Now they had all these new-fangled words to disguise the fact that permanence was out of style. God help us, but these days folks changed "partners" like he changed coats.

'We'll manage, Jos. We always do.'

***

The first letter had arrived many weeks ago. Jos had fingered it cautiously, musing over the South African stamp before reading it. After all this time, it was still hard to believe. Half a lifetime ago, his only sister, Winifred, normally so timid, surprised them all and upped and off, eloped and married in secret to some fellow with a lorry called Barnfather. They'd lived Richmond way for a while, then the next thing anybody knew they were in Cape Town. Apart from a card and letter at Christmas, not much was ever heard, except for the birth of a son, Ambrose, named after his grandfather. That was until four years ago when they had heard the news that Winifred had died. It had been too late and too far to go for the funeral.

The blue airmail letter in Jos's hand was written in a bold italic by someone well versed in the use of language, he reckoned. It was signed, "Your loving nephew, Ambrose".

He was apparently a minister of the church in Bloemfontein, South Africa, who had suddenly found himself invited to attend an Ecumenical Council beginning early in the New Year in London. The upshot was that he had asked if he could stay with his uncle and aunt over Christmas for, having heard all the stories from when he was knee high, he had a yearning to see Keld House and Aunt Emily in particular, after which he would make his way back south for the Council.

After much deliberation, Jos had written back to say that Ambrose would be welcome.

He had enclosed details of train times from London to North Appleton, the nearest station, and a map of the whole area with a ball-point cross marking Keld House above the village.

All had then gone very quiet, almost to a point where the matter had been forgotten, when the next letter arrived from Bloemfontein, confirming that Ambrose would be in North Appleton on December 23rd. He would telephone when he arrived.

A dalesman's soft spot is the loyalty of family, blood ties and hospitality. Jos was no exception and, but for Emmy's fragile state, he would have looked forward to seeing his nephew. Now he was not so sure, but Emily was adamant.

'Shame on you, Jos Robertshaw. A man's word is supposed to be his bond and you've invited him. If you hadn't, then believe you me, Winnie would be turning in her grave.'

'I was only thinking on you, love,' he muttered sheepishly.

The telephone rang suddenly and startlingly. Jos heaved his tall, lean frame out of the chair, walked over and lifted the receiver.

'Robertshaw.'

Brevity was one of his major attributes. He listened, nodding here and there, absent-mindedly noting the bursts of snowflakes drifting past the light outside the window and ending the brief conversation with a desultory, 'Aye, see thee in t'morning then'.

'That were Walter,' he said thoughtfully. 'Apparently he's been trying to get us about pickin' up that stuff from Mason's but t'phone's been out of order. They must have only just got it re-connected.'

A thought suddenly occurred to Emily.

'What if Ambrose arrived early and got himself up here and hasn't been able to get hold of us? Eh dear me, a stranger in a foreign land he's never seen before, let alone knowin' no one, an' to cap it all, snow as well. I hear tell they don't have snow where he comes from.'

'Well lass, whatever, there's not much we can do about it.' Jos scratched his greying head. 'Anyway, wherever he is, surely he'll have had the sense to stay put.'

Emily watched as he wandered over to the window, drew back the curtain and looked out across the yard. There were so many sides to him that she could never quite fathom and, given that, when she thought about it, who ever really knew anyone anyway? What gave people the right to think they understand all the hidden nooks and crannies in a soul, when half the time they don't even know themselves? But, oh, Jos was a steady one. She watched him stooped in the recess of the window, his hands spread along the sill, peering out into the night. She loved the way his hair curled in duck's tails over the oily collar of his jacket. Here was a man who always thought carefully about any decision that had to be made, be it moving sheep down from the high pastures if there was the "smell" of snow on the wind, to deciding which tie to wear with his 'Sunday best' before going on down to the chapel.

'It still can't make up its mind whether to snow us in or keep on pretending,' he muttered. 'Whatever, it ain't worth stayin' up for, that's for sure.'

Of all their memories together, most momentous of all was the day that he proposed to her. The vision of the scene was as sharp-edged in Emily's mind as if it were yesterday, an evening close and heavy, the air thick with the scent of stocks and rose petals drifting up from the garden, and the swallows hunting like arrows amongst the columns of midges above their heads. The clouds were massed along the hillsides that day, heavy with the promise of rain and Jos was ill at ease, shuffling from one foot to the other, torturing and twisting his cap in his hands. Here was a man whose sinewy shoulders could bring the axe whistling down, the sap sticky on the blade as the logs split asunder hour after hour with no visible effect; a man who thought nothing of being out half the night in a blizzard and then emerging in the dawn light with a rescued lamb over his shoulders and his hair and brows crusted with ice.

'I'll just go and do t'rounds,' Jos said then.

He went into the porch, putting on his boots and the old Barbour coat. Clamping a shapeless felt hat on his head, he trod noiselessly over the dry snow. In places the wind had blown the cobbles clean and piled the drifts up against the doors of the toolshed. There was a rattle of steel on steel and Tip and Bess came a chain's length to greet him.

'Na' then, lass.' His weathered hands knew just where to tickle the best places between chin and chest as he unclipped them.

Darting this way and that and running with noses of piled snow they circled him, skittish as young colts. The bond between a farmer and his dog, essentially a working animal who clearly loved the daily round and common task, was something no urban dweller who kept a house pet could ever understand.

He checked the mistel first, the heady syrup scent of hay filling his nostrils and the familiar aroma of contented cattle chewing sporadically, turning their great heads to regard him for a moment. Wandering along the standings, his expert fingers kneaded a cow here and there on the muscles at the root of the tail, which they loved. He was a man totally at one with his animals, using a natural skill, as old as time itself, that understands the mutual language of instinct.

All was well.

He closed the mistel door and, with the windblown snow deeper here, he pushed on past the pigsties. Apart from sporadic grunts, it was quiet. He went on across the garth to the hen houses where his Rhode Island Reds clucked aimlessly on the perches above the deep litter, the nesting boxes lining the walls below them on either side of the hut. By day they scratched and pecked across the field, occasionally "laying away" so that he and Walter had to check the hidden places for eggs. With the advance of dusk he was careful to drop the popholes once the last hen was inside, otherwise the stragglers fell easy prey to the hill foxes. As he crossed to the huts, Tip and Bess were suddenly galvanised, spinning away across the snow, barking madly. Jos noticed the double sets of tracks going from one pophole to another. Two foxes had been testing his defences.

* * *

He recalled the dogs and together they walked over the lower pastures where the sheep, with much wool and lanolin to bar the cold, pulled at stray wisps of hay from the rack in the centre of the field. All was well here, though you could never be too sure. At lambing time the foxes sometimes circled the flocks looking for the chance to dash in and seize the weaklings. If it wasn't the fox, Jos mused, then it was the buzzards or carrion crows. And they went for the eyes first.

He turned and looked back down the rise towards the house, the glowing windows emphasising the snowy landscape, and feeling as he always did that sense of belonging and heritage. He paused, brushing off the snow and resting his arms on the top bar of the gate. A moment of reflection.

He was a man of shrewdness and wisdom when it came to things of the earth, the things that had been in the blood for generations. In his world you never asked for pity when things went wrong or disaster struck. People helped you anyway without being asked. You just did your best to solve the problem yourself, for there were so many things that could go wrong from foot rot in sheep, red mite in hens, swine fever in pigs, and it was always the unexpected that caught you when your back was turned. Invariably, it was linked in some way to the weather, be it gales, floods, blizzards or drought. You had to be vigilant at all times and more often than not it was a combination of sixth sense mixed with knowledge and instinct that saved the day.

Jos loved this land, for it was the land that carried the dust of his ancestors and a fitting monument to their lives. The house had seen the mating, the birthing, the living and the departing of souls against the remote backdrop of world events, news of which in bygone days took forever to reach them, and sometimes never did at all. When the Young Pretender marched out of Scotland and got as far south as Derby in the rebellion of 1745, little realising that, if he had pushed on, he could have easily captured a London emptying in panic, Keld House was already more than a century old. Over a hundred years later, life went on as usual as Bonaparte's armies brought Europe under the yoke of France. A century later the old order changed forever as the villages poured their young men into the bloodbaths of the Somme, Ypres and Passchendaele, in the War to End All Wars. A fine ideal that lasted twenty-one years before it all fell apart again and the distant crump of Nazi bombs could be heard even here, dropping onto the railway marshalling yards of York.

Keld House lived through it all, the only visible signs of change being the slow wearing of the stone by the elements. Attitudes changed and fashions came and went with the shifting tides of opinion but so far the old house had outlasted them all.

From the promise of the spring and the upthrusting of the life force in the earth, to the cry of newborn lambs, so very like the first squalls of a newborn baby, and the scything and cutting of the meadows; this was a world he knew and understood.

Now his breath hung like smoke before being whipped away by the bitter wind, but in his memory he warmed still to that sweet ache of comfort mixed with relief that always followed on the heels of getting in a lap ahead of Mother Nature. When the last bales of hay were safely forked into the loft; when the final load arrived on the laden, squeaking cart just as the thunderheads came in over Dead Man's Hill to lash the earth with liquid stair rods, the hay crop so essential to getting through the winter was secure by just a few moments.

Memories of the long, hot days of summer when sometimes the beck shrank to a trickle and the leaves on the sycamores hung limp and sticky. Sweat in the small of your back and on your brow and the cool relief of a stone-flagged dairy. Those were days when the grass shrivelled and burned, the fellsides shimmered in the heat and milk churns of water were trailered up to the stone troughs for the thirsty animals.

Autumn, he reflected, was his favourite time of all. The fruitful mellowness tinged with sadness for the ageing year and the glories displayed in the reds, golds and browns on the palette of the countryside. Then came the winding down of the land, the last leaves spinning lazily to earth, and the first chilly blasts of the north wind, the winter herald, sighing through the bare bones of the trees.

He had proposed to Emily in autumn. Standing by the gate that evening he looked anywhere but at her, awkward in his suit and polished boots. His hair was newly cut in ragged steps above his ears and plastered down either side of a parting that gleamed like a furrow in a freshly ploughed field. He had been miserable at the apparent hopelessness of it all, the carefully rehearsed lines practised in the mistel day after day had somehow evaporated like puddles in the sun. He stood there forlorn, his great hands still mashing the helpless cap, eyes darting anywhere but in her direction. At last he had forced himself to look at her, the breath seized up in his frame and a hot choking feeling rising in his chest. It was now or never. 'Emily, I bin thinkin...' Then it all got stuck again. 'Well, it's no good!' he had said and thrown the tortured cap over the gate. But she had rescued him. 'Yes, Jos? What about?' His last words had come out in a well nigh unintelligible torrent, but the meaning was true enough. 'I was just wonderin' if we could, well, be together. Would you marry me?' She had never looked so beautiful, poised, holding the bouquet of meadow flowers he had brought her with one hand whilst pushing a strand of chestnut hair from the fullness of her mouth with the other. The grey-blue eyes danced, her breasts taut beneath the cotton dress and all the lissom wonder of a young girl in her prime. 'Well, Jos Robertshaw, I thought you were never going to ask. Of course I'll marry you.'

Sweet memory. And the time later, scrubbed, ruddy-cheeked and with his collar pinching painfully, standing beside Emily in the little chapel at Nethergill singing lustily, 'All is safely gathered in...' The day they were married.

Emily. He broke from his reverie, whistled up the dogs and hurried down the track to the house. Kicking the snow from his boots, he hung the Barbour on the broom handle. Lifting the latch he peered into the living room. She was asleep, a stray wisp of hair across the waxen face. The fire in the range had burned down to a dull glow. The lamplight winked back and forth among the horse brasses on the lintel, and the only sound was the keening wind hunting across the frozen windowpanes.

Gently he whispered in her ear, and folding his arms about her, he easily lifted the quiet form and carried her up the worn stone steps to bed.

Chapter 2

_____

MONDAY 23 DECEMBER

IT WAS Monday morning at the farm, and the day that Ambrose Barnfather was supposed to arrive in North Appleton. The snow had ceased, giving way to a day of blinding white with sunshine from a steely blue sky. The wind still came from the north with a keen razor edge and throughout the day the temperature barely lifted above freezing. Icicles hung like organ pipes from the guttering of the mistel. The boulders in the beck were sugar-coated with frozen spray and fingers of snow still clung to the telephone wires.

Jos and Walter had begun their day as ever, milking, with breath rising in smoky clouds from man and beast. The cows were fothered and turned out while they mucked out and washed down. The tractor, known affectionately as Old Beelzebub, sat ticking over in the yard while the heavy milk churns were loaded onto the trailer.

The big back wheels of the tractor with their heavy tread tyres bit easily into the snow on the upward winding lane. But Jos frequently had to wipe the tears from his eyes as he peered into the scything wind.

Tip and Bess ranged across the snow as free spirits, here one minute and gone the next, but ready to return to Jos at a word or whistle. The same old routine, seven days a week, over the cattle grid at the top and roll the churns on to the platform to await collection. How many times had he done this? Countless. He noted the road had been ploughed. It had to be; it was vital to get the milk wagons through. He was about to turn back down the lane when he spotted the familiar red Post Office Land Rover grinding up the hill.

Laurie Bean had seen a lifetime at the job, through every kind of weather and situation.

He was a law unto himself and a hot-wire into all the gossip which, largely thanks to him, circulated swiftly.

'Na then, Jos, bit slape this morning,' he bellowed over the combined racket of two wheezing diesels.

'I'll give you t'post an' it'll save me a run. I'm late enough as it is.'

He slipped the rubber bands off the bundle of letters, thumbing through the Christmas mail, assorted bills and accounts, and Jos's *Yorkshire Post*. In the middle of the bundle was a postcard liberally spattered with palm trees and bikini clad girls. Jos turned it over several times viewing it this way and that.

'Oh, that,' said Laurie, 'That's from someone called Claire who's a friend of Arnold's, on holiday with someone called Anton in Florida. Sent care of you.'

'Really?' Jos eyed the postman with a baleful look. 'Tha's got to be t'nosiest bugger around.'

Laurie grinned,

'Well, you 'ave to keep abreast of the times you know.'

The back of his Land Rover was jammed to the roof with Christmas trees and boxes of groceries that gave out the cheerful clink of bottles. The Post Office would not have approved but the old folk of the high country certainly did, unable to get out as so many of them were, and it ensured Laurie a rich supply of whiskies, beers, sherries, obligatory mince pies and, in most places, coins pressed into his welcoming palm with a muttered,

'Compliments of the season.'

"Ave you heard owt of t'lad from South Africa then?'

Jos shook his head. 'He's supposed to be arrivin' at 'Appleton today.'

'You be thrang this Christmas then?'

Laurie had an unquenchable thirst for the details of people's lives that bordered on the obsessive.

'Aye. Counting Walter and Laura, there'll be seven of us on Christmas Day.'

'How's Emily keepin?'

A fleeting cloud passed across Jos's face.

'Oh, tha knows, fair to middlin'. It can only be expected.'

The postman bade him farewell with a grinding of gears and clouds of blue diesel smoke.

***

Jos drove on back down towards the farm, parking in the lee of the mistel. He climbed down from the tractor, unhitched the trailer and then walked off into the house with the post.

Emily was sitting in her chair by the fire while Laura was by the dresser ironing, the pleasant smell of hot, crisp linen filling the room. Jos went over to kiss his wife gently on the cheek.

'No word from t'nephew then?' he queried, pouring boiling water from the ever ready kettle on the hob over a strainer full of tea leaves, adding four teaspoons of sugar and a splash of milk from the can on the table. The tea, soundly stirred, had a dark soup-like consistency and, blowing on it between gulps, he soon drained to the bottom.

'No, and not likely neither', Laura said bluntly.

'We've just tried to call Harkers for some bits and pieces and t'line's dead again. Walter reckons it's ice on t'wires bringin' them down.'

'That's all we need,' Jos grumbled. He took his empty mug into the kitchen and headed for the door. 'There's nowt we can do so I'd best be gettin' on.'

'I suppose,' said Emily, 'If he does get to Appleton and he can let us know, you'll be going for him in the Land Rover?'

He paused in mid stride, 'Well... aye.'

'Then it might be a good idea to tidy it up a bit because knowing you it'll be full of junk. There'll be no room for t'lad.'

He walked out into the yard muttering under his breath. 'Women. Sometimes fit to craze a saint.'

With his nephew uppermost in his thoughts and knowing better than to argue with Emily, ill or not, Walter and he attempted to give the inside of the Land Rover a face lift. They removed bags and bales, assorted bundles of twine and paper bags, tools, a roll of barbed wire, a sledge hammer, boxes of nails, several storm lanterns, a jerry can of paraffin and,

31

puzzlingly, a single cricket pad with the straps
chewed off.

'You wonder where all this stuff comes
from,' said Walter to no one in particular.

The vehicle had also been parked under a
standing by the mistel and unbeknown to Jos
had just been taken over as home by one of
the farm cats. From a bag of wood shavings
in the back he and Walter had gingerly carried
four squalling kittens to a bed on an old army
greatcoat in the hay loft.

***

The day stayed fine and clear. Apart from a
break for the mid-day meal they spent most of
the time cutting logs. The iron saw bench had
a great circular blade greased with goose fat
when not in use and driven by a belt that ran
from a pulley on the tractor.

Autumn did a lot of the initial work. As
October gave way to November, the onslaught
of the winter gales finished off the process of
life, death and decay and the wind brought
the dead and dying timber to the ground.

Sometimes it was the whole tree. An oak could have up to six miles of roots and its timber prodigiously strong, but if the ground was frozen hard then beeches and elms in particular were weakened and could go down under the immense pressure of the wind. Myriad plants and organisms that flourished in the long days of summer faded and died to form the nourishment for the same process the following year. The tree produced its splendid canopy of leaves only to shed them in the "back end" to add to the leaf mould beneath that gave strength and sustenance to feed the tree. With the aid of the earth, it fed itself. The key to the mystery of life lay in there somewhere.

Among Keld House Farm's several hundred acres were two small woods, all that remained of the forest that would have covered much of the land hundreds of years before. Up on the fellside were several breaks of pine trees and a copse around the ruined lime kiln.

Jos and Walter would chainsaw the deadfall timber brought down by the gales and trailer it back to the farm. Walter mistrusted the chainsaw but it was easier than the old days

33

when they cut the wood by hand with a great two-handed saw six feet in length.

In the shed, as they worked on, floured by the flying clouds of sawdust and half deafened by the shrill whine of the circular blade, the woodpile outside, seasoned by the weather, diminished and the pyramid of logs grew higher, spilling out across the floor.

It was a great way of keeping warm and when the pile of wood was of sufficient height the tractor was shut down and the leather belt looped over the rafters. Then each got to work on the chopping blocks, two waist-high sections of tree trunk, their tops worn and grooved with the impact of countless steel edges. As old Ambrose had told Jos long ago,

'Listen, lad, and think on, tha' can't split logs with a sharp blade. It does nowt but stick in t'wood.' So Walter used a blunt tree axe, Jos a wedge-shaped splitter. There was a rhythm in the work that used no more energy than was necessary; the drum of timber lifted up onto the block, the axe head descending more by its own weight than powered by flailing muscles and the deeply satisfying thunk and rending split as the steel parted the wood.

The logs were neatly stacked until all the available space in the building was full. Ash logs were by far the best for they burned green or old. Birch logs had tar in their bark which made them an excellent firelighter, whilst Cherry scented a room. Elm, the crossgrained wood that blunted many a saw, smouldered with hardly a flame while Pine was just the opposite and banged and cracked loudly, firing red hot missiles into the room. Sycamore lasted briefly while the noble Beech burned for hours.

***

It was now mid-afternoon and already the blue shadows behind the walls were starting to lengthen. Walter stretched his aching back and glanced up at the sky. 'It's still clear enough.'

Jos watched him carefully putting away the tools. For so many years with hardly the feeling of "boss" and "employee" they had worked side by side. They knew to depend on one another and if there was a difference of opinion then it

35

was never allowed to linger, for in such lay the destruction of a working relationship and the erosion of respect. They both understood that. They also understood with the gift of hindsight that in their particular world there could be few secrets. Between them, their knowledge of farming, and hill farming in particular, was encyclopaedic. What one did not know then, like as not, the other would.

And then there was the business with Emily. From the day they realised that things could not get any better, only worse, Walter had been a rock to him. Little unassuming kindnesses, shrugged self-effacingly away. So often taking the major workload on his shoulders so that the boss could devote more time to his wife and adding unpaid hours to his six-day working week to help keep things going. Then there was Laura, who had taken it upon herself to run Keld House. Jos had tried once to say, stumblingly, just how much he appreciated all Walter had done. The other had blushed under his wind-tanned face and edged away, muttering something about how Jos had always seen him right and such things didn't have to be said. It was never alluded to again.

Still, Jos felt for all his years that he was standing on the edge of the unknown. It would not be long before he would be alone. The thought frightened him and filled him with a cold terror. Could he even stomach trying to keep the farm going? Would he be, like so many others, heartbroken and shell-shocked at the sudden collapse of a way of life stretching back down centuries? Would he end up where he did not want to be, in a house in North Appleton with his very soul crying out for the sound of the curlews on the moorland, and the rush of the clean wind in the sycamores?

He was a gentle man but there were times he wanted to destroy those who were driving the hill farmer over and beyond the stark edges of reason. And all in the name of progress.

He had always been brought up to be honest and, wherever possible, treat others as he would like to be treated himself, in the sure and certain knowledge that life is hard and nobody owes you a living. But nobody seemed to think like that any more and the past was a dirty word.

And Walter? He watched him disappear with an axe into the tool store. What would become of him? The farm had been his whole life, the very compass of his world. Could he ever look him in the eyes and tell him, 'It's finished?'

Could they make a go of it together? He doubted it for, heaven help him, with the passing of Emily, then in more senses than one, the spirit would be gone. It was too late for both of them, for the balance was destroyed and too much of what was happening now was only relevant to a young man's world with no survivors if you were over the hill. Too late to "diversify" – whatever *that* was supposed to mean.

Still, life did go on and no point in thinking like this when it was Christmas time, supposedly with glad tidings of great joy. Like all his generation, he had learned the Catechism at his mother's knee, and attended Sunday School for the strengthening of the spiritual "backbone". It was neither simply a case of habit nor of tradition, for folks then believed in the strengthening of the soul.

The body was mortal and built for toil and consequently could take care of itself.

He was not an overtly religious man in terms of regular church attendance, nor did he make ostentatious expressions of faith. His relationship with his Maker was one of humble respect at the might and mystery of nature, quietly spoken thanks when the harvest was home and an acceptance of Emily's condition as he would accept the often harsh elements of the natural world. It all seemed to be thrown into starker relief at Christmas.

Christmas! Jos suddenly remembered his missing nephew. He'd hardly spared him a thought.

He hurried across the yard into the house.

Chapter 3

THE SAME DAY

THE SHADOWS moved across the snow from the walls and occasional trees, lengthening as the afternoon stretched on with increasing speed to meet the frost-crackling, star-spangled velvet dusk.

The snow had been blown deep on either side of the track and beaten down on the rough road by the tractor wheels, while the wind moaned around the electricity wires slung from post to post down the fields to eventually disappear from view into the ghyll.

Wires indicated a house.

The tall figure stood outlined against the late afternoon sky. He remained quite still for a moment, taking in the scene before him and noting the name on the gate in the wall.

He smiled, nodded to himself then, adjusting the strap of his holdall, strode on down the track towards Keld House Farm.

Above his head the moon rode out from behind the clouds like a great silver ship, close-hauled on her voyage across the night sky, while the frost, nipping ears and fingers, came down harder than ever.

Chapter 4

LATER THAT SAME DAY

JOS HAD tried the phone again. It was still dead. Laura had spent the afternoon cleaning the house thoroughly and had pushed Emily in her chair over to the table. One thing was certain, she hated to be idle. There was the goose to stuff, more pies to fill with mince and plenty to keep her busy. Jos was worried, pacing around the pair, running his hands through his hair, a sure sign that he was agitated.

'What's to be done about nephew? Do you think I ought to go on up to North Appleton and see if he's pitched up at all?'

'No point in that. It's a fair way to go for a wasted journey.' As ever Emily was the right side of reason. 'He's a big lad by now.'

'Well, no use worryin', I suppose. Milkin' time.'

He picked up the milk can and opened the door into the porch, absentmindedly shuffling his stockinged feet into his boots, gazing across the yard to where the familiar wedge of light spilled out onto the snow from the mistel. The low contented murmurings of the cows, the putt-putting of the milking machine mixed with Walter's whistling and the clang of milk churns on concrete was no different to any other day in the year, but something else was decidedly odd, and it took a few moments to sink in.

A tall figure was standing to one side of the yard, reaching down to Tip and Bess and rubbing their ears. They were the best watchdogs in the world and nobody could do that until they had been thoroughly barked at, suspiciously sniffed at, vetted and subjected to Jos's approval. Jos walked forward, then came to an abrupt halt, totally forgetting himself. 'Well I'll be damned.'

'I sincerely hope not.' The voice was

humorous, warm and rich, the clipped accent strongly flavoured with Afrikaans. 'You must be Jos.'

The smile was wide, set in the tanned face. Dark hair fell to the collar and the outstretched hand that gripped Jos's was firm and strong.

'That I am,' he replied, taken completely off his guard. 'And you must be Winnie's lad. I can see the resemblance.'

The young man said nothing. Just the enigmatic smile and the two standing regarding one another, caught up in the moment and tongue-tied. Jos came to his senses. 'Nay, lad, I'm forgettin' meself. You must be nithered, come on in and welcome to Keld House.'

'Thank you.' They crossed the yard, Jos with the sense of awkwardness that comes from a lifetime of rarely seeing people from the outside world. In the porch, kicking off the boots he'd only just put on, he lowered his voice to a whisper. 'Your aunt is not what she used to be, Ambrose. It just gets slowly worse.'

He unsnecked the door and pushed it open. The young man stood in the doorway, blinking in the light. The smell of baking wafted from the oven and the kettle sniffled little puffs of steam on the hob. The newcomer noted the beamed ceiling and the way the lamplight played on the brasses and copper warming pan.

A lady with a round homely face and an apron bearing the legend, "I am the Boss", was sitting at one end of a laden table polishing a brass candlestick. In another chair at the same table sat someone whose face was so familiar to him. The features were thinned and ravaged by the disease, but the intense blue eyes were very much alive.

'We have a visitor,' said Jos with a triumphant flourish of his arm, like a magician pulling a rabbit out of the hat. 'Ambrose Barnfather in person.'

'Oh, oh well I never. You got here at last.' Emily looked up at the young face almost disbelievingly.

'We've been fair mithered about you what with the phones being dead an' all and the weather so cold.' The words came spilling out like beans from a sack. 'And Jos wondering if he ought to go and get you and ... and ... oh,

I just don't believe it, Winnie's boy, and my, you've grown since then.'

She pointed to a colour photograph on the dresser of a fat, smiling baby playing with a tape measure on a lawn. 'Winnie sent us that when you were three.'

The young man smiled and walked over to her. Usually Emmy was acutely aware of her condition and felt an undeserved shame when someone other than Jos or Laura came into her world. It was strange that she did not feel like that with this suntanned visitor although he had been in the house just a few moments.

She brushed aside a stray wisp of hair and looked up at him as he bent and kissed her cheek. He was so very tall, she thought, the grey eyes filled with kindness and a certain compassion but also something unfathomable, something way beyond all that. It was most likely to do with his vocation, the added strength, depth and wisdom that comes of devotion to things of the spirit, and ministering to every kind of need. And all in one so young.

'Get your coat off lad, and come and sit by

t'fire and get those bones of yours warmed through.'

Jos introduced him to Laura, who had recovered her composure from the first shock of the tanned stranger appearing through the door, wiped her hands on her apron and shook his proffered hand firmly.

It was all bustle and fuss. The Robertshaws were modest people who saw very few visitors other than the local folk and there was a sense of awkwardness to overcome.

Winifred had left in the night all those years ago, never to return, her bones in the soil of a far off land. Here was her son, their nephew, newly arrived.

Jos carried his bag to the stair bottom before the question occurred to him. 'How on earth did you get here?'

'Well,' he said seemingly at ease already, 'finding myself at the other end of the country, I made a few enquiries and one way and another I got myself up to North Appleton.' He paused to take a sip of his tea, allowing no change of expression to cross his face as he swallowed the scalding liquid, and continued.

'The journey was not exactly straightforward. The weather was causing all kinds of problems and I didn't get to North Appleton until after lunch. I tried calling you but just got a strange sound so, thinking that it might be something to do with the snow, I got out your map, figured out my route and set off hitching up the road.'

'Aye, lad, in this weather an' all.' Jos shook his head. 'It must have been a right shock after South Africa. I'll bet you near froze to death.'

'I got very cold waiting for the first lift, in a baker's van, would you believe, but with the heater on full blast he soon thawed me out. He was a nice fellow who offered me coffee from his flask and pointed things out as we came up into the hill country.'

He paused again as if renewing the recent events of his journey, the unspoken thoughts passing over his face like cloud patterns on a hillside. He continued, 'I love the way the snow blankets everything and yet you can still see the shape and style of the villages clustered round their churches and pubs. Wonderful. Anyway, my lift had to turn off in Coneystone.

I said, 'goodbye and thank you,' and was prepared for a long wait when, as luck would have it, a vet picked me up on his way back from a farm and dropped me off in the village. He would even have run me up here because he said he knows you well, but he was already late for surgery. I was quite happy to walk it.'

'Was it a Land Rover? And did he have a beard?' Laura had no compunction about asking.

'Yes he did.'

'Aye, that would be Jim Slater. Married, two nippers an' lives in the big house behind Walter and me. Good vet. Likes a pint, mark you, and tells terrible jokes, but never backwards at comin' forwards when somebody needs him.'

Walter! With the relief flooding through him now that his nephew was safely here Jos had forgotten that Walter was out there in a freezing cow shed on his own. Nothing unusual these days but he hadn't even told him about the visitor.

Excusing himself, he put on his boots and headed across the yard. Any misgivings he might have had about his nephew landing on

49

them for Christmas had melted away in the few minutes spent together, although he had to admit he could not really make the lad out. He paused in the shadow of the mistel and looked back at the glowing windows of the house. Emily was out of his field of vision but he could make out his nephew, mug of tea still clasped in his hands, standing with his back to the fire.

***

Laura had cleared a space among the chaos on the table. Milking finished, Jos had brought Walter in to meet the visitor. After an initial muttered, 'How d'ya do,' he wrapped himself around a tankard of "lotion", adding it was 'for t'road'. Nobody seemed to mind that he brought a liberal helping of the aromas of the cowshed with him and Jos hadn't seen Emily so "fired up", as he put it, in months.

The young visitor missed nothing as he quietly observed the scene before him. He noticed how these people in their way cared one for another. Even Walter, for all his laconic facade, was clearly a man with more under his skin than met the eye.

The subject of milking came up and the young man said he would rather like to see that. Walter couldn't fathom that at all. 'Nay, these days there's nowt to it. Tha' should have been around a few years ago. We did it all by hand then, none of this sit back and wait for t'machine lark. Them were t'days.'

He finished his beer, reckoned he'd see Jos in the morning as usual, bade the visitor and Emily, 'G'night,' and set off with Laura in his little green van, the metallic rattle of snow chains audible long after they had disappeared into a fold of the hills.

***

The three of them sat around the table long after the meal was over, for in the old farmhouses that was ever the way of things. Before the power lines brought electricity to the Dales, it was a world of lamps and candles in the evenings and television unknown. The day's news and doings would be discussed, gossip related and, embellished wherever possible, and clothes mended by lamplight, eggs washed and papers read before retiring early to bed.

They had eaten a simple meal prepared in part by Emily and cooked by Laura before she left. The young man was asked to say Grace, which he did, giving thanks for the meal and the good people who provided it, their heads bowed in the solemnity of the moment. Steak and kidney pie followed with cauliflower, green beans and potatoes and apple and rhubarb under a mouth-watering crust for pudding.

Jos took two pewter tankards from the dresser and wandered off into the stone larder behind the kitchen. It was dimly lit by one small window by day and at night by a naked bulb on the beam above. Flitches of ham twirled slowly on iron hooks above sides of bacon curing in salt on the stone slabs below.

His keg of "lotion" sat on two trestles by the steps, while around the walls the shelves were lined with every kind of fruit and vegetable bottled in screwtop jars. He paused in the doorway as if having forgotten something.

'Er, nephew, I was going to get you a beer.

Never thought to ask, you bein' a minister an' all.'

'If it was good enough for Cana in Galilee, then it is good enough for me,' the other smiled, sitting in the "comfy" chair opposite Emily.

They sat around the fire, the men with their beer, Emily, arms folded on her lap, and the time skipped on. Jos thought his nephew seemed disinclined to go deep into family matters. Maybe it was the newness of it all, the shock of landing slap in the middle of a place and folks he'd never seen in his life and only knew by reputation. After all, he thought, how would he feel when home was twelve thousand miles away? The old man was too polite to press his nephew for details. Maybe, as Winifred had died so recently, the young man found the subject too painful. There were so many questions. What of life back there in that faraway land? What was it like? Had his mother and George Barnfather been happy? What was his father doing now? At one point Jos asked a direct question about the Mission in Bloemfontein.

'More of that later,' the other replied, watching Emily sipping a cup of hot milk. 'At least I'm here and there is time enough for reminiscing.'

Jos then spoke at length, with interjections from Emily as to the exact times of dates, about the family's past. Normally a man of few words, he spoke in a slow deep voice, the measured cadences of the words enriched with the warmth of the north country accent.

It was clear that he had always felt quite protective about his sister, and her sudden disappearance with young Barnfather all those years ago was still something that baffled him for it was outside his range of comprehension. His father too, had found Winifred's's elopement hard to come to terms with. 'If only we'd known more then maybe we could have understood it more, but the old lad was very fixed in his opinions. Once his mind was made up that was it and heaven and earth could not shake him,' he said.

'The very Devil himself would have failed,' said Emily, with a feeling, obviously based on experience.

'He was as solid as a rock.'

'On the other hand,' Jos chewed his lip thoughtfully, 'though Old Ambrose, who you never knew could be an awkward soul and on occasions downright unreasonable, deep down I think he was impressed that she called you after him. Heaven knows she had no reason to.'

The young man sat listening and Jos thought him either to be quite shy, not in his opinion a great attribute for a minister, or overawed by the relatively strange world of the farm.

For a while, all was silent but for the measured ticking of the grandfather clock and the occasional thud from the fire as, with an accompanying shower of sparks, the spent embers dropped through on to the grate beneath. Jos shuffled his feet and stared at a point on the stone-flagged floor with exaggerated attention. 'Aye, well,' he said at last, 'she'll be right enough now, lad. Tha's done as she wished. You're here.'

Emily was mortally tired, Jos could see. This had been a momentous day for her and maybe too much excitement was a dangerous thing. The eyes were still bright but there were definite signs of weariness as the waves of pain and discomfort were making their inexorable way through her thin frame. It was much later than she would normally have stayed up.

'Time for t'rounds, lass.' He rose stiffly to his feet.

'Maybe you'd like to go with him then? That is if you're not too tired, it being freezin' an' all,' she added.

'Certainly.'

The young man had been watching Emily, noting the brave face she put on a seemingly hopeless situation. He remained thoughtful whilst donning his long coat and muffler.

***

The two men crossed the yard together, the frost crystals crunching like powdered glass beneath their feet. It was, as Jos put it, cold enough to "curdle your marrow". Their breath hung about them as if loath to leave and the skies were clear, the Milky Way filled with stars. Tip and Bess came out of their barrel houses wriggling with delight in anticipation of having their heads rubbed and chests tickled. The young man reached down and rubbed his fingers in their fur. Jos unclipped them and they spun away across the snow.

The two men wandered from building to building.

Jos was in his element now, on his home turf, surrounded by all that he knew and cared for. He explained to his nephew how the farm worked, how all the patterns dovetailed into the seasons, all of it logical, with the natural world balancing itself, weeding out the weak and providing for the strong.

At one point they were standing by the midden, the ammonia-laden smell blanketed by the coating of frozen snow. Jos explained how they took manure out on to the fields in the "front end" of the year to soak the richness down into the earth to boost the hay meadows. Like the tree being fed with its own dying leaves, everything had its place in the rhythm of life.

The round complete, they came back down the field towards the house, its windows glowing in the night. Jos stopped, leaning as he always did on the top bar of the gate. The young man stood silently beside him taking in the winter world.

'It's all I've ever known, lad.' Jos's voice was soft and low. 'You've got Robertshaw blood in your veins. It's still a part of you and I'm glad you got over 'ere to see us, but I think our times are coming to an end. Your aunt ain't going to get better. You can see that. An' Walter an' me, well, let's just say the times have changed far more than us. Arnold ain't interested in the farm and I, for one, can't see no way forward. It all seems like it was for nothin.'

It was as if the veil were suddenly lifted from the quietly enigmatic young man of the past few hours and he spoke with a measured authority that wriggled under Jos's defences like a bird beneath a wire.

'How do you mean, all for nothing?'

The old man was about to set off into a speech about the downhill slide but the timbre of the young man's voice had an edge that stopped Jos's words on his lip. 'I have been here only a few hours and, relative or not, to all intents and purposes a stranger in your midst because you don't really know me. I'm a stranger from a far away place.'

He rested his elbows on the gate beside Jos. 'Try to forget for a moment, who or what I am supposed to be. Perhaps it is difficult to understand exactly what I am saying because you're so close to things, but I see here a little world which in its completeness and honesty and closeness to the earth and the natural harmony, stands as a signpost to something durable and fine. It is like the threads which, when pulled together, form the essence of the cloth.'

'There is a goodness here that is all the better for being a part of the natural course of events, rather than something contrived. I doubt that anyone coming down to this place in need of care and help would be turned away.'

Jos was silent.

'Tonight – as we talked in the house – you said you felt awkward because here I am, having just crossed half the world in a few hours and you always regarded a trip into Langthwaite as an outing. That was as far as you ever went, you said, except for one day trip to York long ago. It seemed to me that you felt inadequate on account of that; that your horizons were too narrow.'

He paused momentarily.

'I don't see anything wrong with being in the centre of your world when people are flying so far and so fast that half the time they don't know who they are, where they're going or where they've been.'

Jos felt as if his very soul was being dissected and scrutinized and bits of him spread around like pieces of a jigsaw puzzle on the parlour table. It put him on the defensive, nettled but intrigued. He muttered half heartedly, 'It were mostly work in them days. There weren't much time for owt else an' then I met Emily, started courting and that were it. Things are different now'.

'But if you think about it,' the other continued, 'the earthshakers, the people who changed the past and affected our lives to this day, they were never high-rollers. They tended to be simple ordinary people, farmers like yourself, and fishermen; people who worked close to the earth and the elements.'

'There's a whole world out there that has forgotten what this season is really all about, the mystery of Christmas. It is based on an earth-shaking event when a child was born into the most wretched of circumstances but changed the course of history and much more.'

'You have a quality here that has gone from other places. There is a peace that others have driven from their world, as if they are scared to face themselves in the silence.'

Jos shuffled his booted feet on the packed snow. He'd never heard folks talk like this and the clipped accent and sureness of delivery was almost irritating, a bit like them clever so-and-sos on TV, full of their own importance and listening to no one but themselves. And yet. And yet... He knew in his bones that the young man was right, and he, Jos Robertshaw, after all these years was losing faith in himself and his way. God alone knew he had enough reason, but just when he'd got himself convinced that all was up, along comes this young upstart, who he hardly knows, telling him something different.

He felt ashamed that he could think of his nephew in this way and for the second time that day he was taken aback and did not know what to make of it.

The other paused for a moment. 'You see no way forward, but what is forward? To make more money and then more, and more? How many of those so-called "forward" people know how to look backward? To enjoy just rewards is fair enough, but to chase the crock of gold at the end of the rainbow for its own sake? Where does that get you in the end?'

His nephew's face was almost unearthly in the light from the night sky. 'You have a great phrase here, that a shroud has no pockets.'

He weighed his words carefully, watching Jos's expression.

'When you are so troubled and carry the burden that you do, I hope you will pardon me for saying it, but to me you seem very complete here when so many folk with so much, worry themselves into an early grave striving for more.'

He could see that Jos was unused to this kind of rhetoric; that he was confused and agitated. The old man was nobody's fool but he clearly liked to savour a point of view and give it some time to settle. His natural wisdom was a philosophy born of a lifetime in the measured pace of the natural order, not slick arguments. Most importantly of all, he carried the unspeakable burden of impending loss.

They walked on down to the house in silence. Jos chained Tip and Bess then both men took off their boots in the porch. He pushed the door slowly ajar, slipping through into the warm room. The fire had sunk low in the gate and Emily was asleep, her face pale, her eyes shadowed. Her hands were open on her lap, turned slightly upwards as if in supplication to some benign power.

The rug had slipped from her knees to the floor.

The old man turned to look at his nephew. Nothing was said, no move was made, but his unspoken words seemed to cry aloud between the walls, the unsounded words of a man watching the most precious being he had ever known being torn slowly but surely away from him. All the fine words in the world, all the clever sayings, could not alter that.

He walked over to her chair, leaving the young man standing quietly by the table. The silence was the silence of an old house, comfortable with the fact, its walls used to the quality, drawn down through four hundred years. Parties, arguments and gettogethers might be raucous, boisterous affairs, but then the silence would return like waves running in on the sand, restoring an equanimity and balance to the senses. It was something not to be feared and driven away but welcomed, more often than not as a comfort and balm to the toil of the day.

Jos bent down and, as ever, touched his wife's cheek. His hands, so calloused and rough from contact with wood, stone and weather, had the gentleness of thistledown.

His nephew, his grey eyes deep as a bottomless pool, watched. There were words that could be said, but no words were necessary.

Gently, Jos lifted her, holding the precious form to him, as a child would hold a rag doll.

The young man moved to the door at the bottom of the stairs and lifted the sneck. For a second the eyes of the two men held each to the other in a moment of shared understanding.

Jos went carefully up the stairs, looking down with each upward step at the ravaged face that had not even woken. One day soon, he knew, the face would sleep forever.

He carried her into her room.

Later he came downstairs again. The young man was still standing, gazing into the dying embers of the fire.

'You have pain enough. I hope you don't think I went too far.'

'Think nowt on it, lad. It's been this way for some time. Let me show you up to your room.'

As they passed Emily's room, the door was ajar and a candle burned on a bedside table. Jos had laid her hair neatly across the pillow and the young man realized that he had brushed it. The face was sunk in repose.

Jos opened another door off the landing. A beam ran the length of the ceiling, the floor timbers were of polished pine with one rag rug, the window looked down to the snowy yard and another candle burned at the bedside.

'We still use candles a lot,' he whispered. 'Old habits an' all that.'

The young man's bag had been put by the bed and on the pine chest by the bedside an old Delft jug of water, basin and towel and a leather Bible with brass clasps lay alongside.

'Remember if tha' gets a bit cold there's more covers in t'chest, oh, and yes, there's hangers for your clothes in t'cupboard,' said Jos, indicating a tall pine cabinet in the corner. Jos stood awkwardly, unsure of what to say next.

'Goodnight then.'

'Goodnight.'

His figure retreated down the long upper corridor of Keld House. The young man watched him disappear into a side room.

The moon sailed on behind islands of windblown cloud beyond the window and the familiar silence settled on the night. For a long time he remained motionless, the light bathing his face. Then, walking to the window, he raised his hands in solemn supplication to the heavens.

Chapter 5

TUESDAY, 24 DECEMBER

HE WOKE to the lowing of cattle across the yard.

As he lay looking up at the beamed ceiling, the white light reflecting from the snow outside was almost dazzling. He washed with a sharp intake of breath, splashing the icy water from the jug over his face and could not help but notice that there were fernlike patterns of frost on the inside of the windows.

Down in the yard the cattle, their heads nodding in easy symmetry, were plodding on their unhurried way to the big shed where they spent the winter. The entire landscape seemed coated in white sugar and with the full light he

Chris Simpson

was able to see just how snugged down into the hills Keld House was. Walter's van was parked in its usual place next to the log store and he could see Jos wheeling barrowloads of manure out to the midden, the steam rising in dense clouds in the freezing air. They must have been up for two or three hours.

A mouth-watering smell of cooking was drifting up from the downstairs kitchen.

He made his way down past Emily's room, noting that the door was shut, and stepped into the living room. Festive music spilled from a radio over by the settle.

Laura had an array of pans on the range, the fire glowing with new life and, he noted, the wood box full of fresh, split logs. The table had been partially cleared again and four places set with a new wholemeal loaf on the bread board.

'Good morning,' he ventured, as an upbeat version of 'The Holly and the Ivy' seeped from the speakers of the radio.

'Mornin',' she smiled at him. 'Sleep well?'

'I did. The first thing I knew it was morning.'

'First thing I knew,' said Laura, briskly

stirring a pan of what appeared to be broken eggs, 'Walter is on his back snoring fit to blow t'walls out and it's time to get stirrin' again. Felt like we'd hardly got to bed. It does get cold hereabouts in winter, but I 'ave to say I thought to misen as we came down t'lane, we might just as well be at t'North Pole.'

He smiled.

'Can you bring me that plate?' She nodded towards the dresser. He followed her into the larder where she reached up and lifted the ham from the hook. Laying it down on a slab, she sliced the rashers with an expertise born of long practice and he carefully hung the flitch back up again when she decided that she had cut enough. Together they went back into the kitchen.

The eggs went on a big dish into the oven, "egg scrimmage" she called it, while mushrooms and tomatoes went into the pan with the ham. Fried bread followed with slices of black pudding, made in the village. He could not believe the volume of food until it occurred to him that the two frozen individuals out there in the farm had begun work in the pitch dark, and in the dead of winter. Tea was made and left to "mash".

'That's about it,' she said, wiping a pink brow. 'Give 'em a yell.'

'What about Emily?' he ventured, but she looked up at the ceiling and made a finger-on-the-lips motion, shaking her head. 'She doesn't get up that early these days. Best let her rest awhile.'

He had not even got to the door when he heard voices and the stamping of rubber boots in the porch. The door swung open, bringing a chilly blast of winter undershot with the fragrance of the cowshed. Red-faced and noses sniffing in the warmth, Jos and Walter sat down.

Between, 'Mornin',' and, 'Sleep well?' and a good-natured, 'It's all right for some,' directed at the visitor, they set about cutting great doorstops of bread. The hot plates were on the table, the iron pans of cooked breakfast placed on mats and everyone helped themselves. In his whole existence he had never tasted anything so good and any doubts he may have had concerning the actual consumption of the food were quickly dispelled.

Apart from the festive radio, silence reigned, interspersed with munching and the rattle of cutlery. At length, after an audible sigh of pleasure, Jos made to wipe his mouth on the back of his hand then, remembering his guest, used his sleeve instead.

The talk was of what was to be done that day.

Winter closed everything in and no one would be venturing far over the fells, but there were still things to be done. Re-fuelling, bringing down more fother from the barn, kindling and logs and preparing foodstuffs for the animals.

'Do you fancy 'avin' a look round, nephew?' There was no trace of the anguish of the previous night, just a certain knowledge behind the eyes.

'Well, yes. I just don't want to get in the way.'

'Not much chance of that. We have to firstly get the milk up t'lane then grab some holly on t'way back, what with all the keltement coming on Christmas Day.'

Everyone took their plates over to the sink in the kitchen. Walter headed out again after a surreptitious belch that earned him a sharp rebuke from Laura, and the young man got his coat and muffler.

'Try these for size. I reckon they're about you.' Jos handed him a pair of rubber boots. He found that they fitted his stockinged feet remarkably well. Once out into the yard he was astonished at just how cold it was.

Apparently the phone was still dead and looking up at the wires there was no wonder, for they sparkled with ice crystals. Cold or not, he had to concede that it was incredibly beautiful. The hills ranged about them like great pillows, smoothed by the crisp blanket of snow and under the blue sky everything shimmered in a blinding white light.

While Jos went to start the tractor and shackle up the trailer, he wandered down through the garden with Tip and Bess leaping about him. The shrubs were twice their normal size under overcoats of snow, and the branches of the fruit trees picked out in a delicate tracery of ice. Bird tracks and cats' paw prints led down to the beck which still tinkled between boulders in their glassy coats.

The distant roar of Beelzebub firing into life prompted him to hurry back up to the yard. He clambered onto the tractor beside Jos and with a grinding of gears and a shattering racket from the exhaust pipe that sent clouds of startled rooks rocketing up out of the sycamores, they swung out of the yard and up onto the farm road. The trailer followed obediently behind with its complement of milk churns and they climbed up out of the Ghyll, the cold air stinging their faces and the big wheels throwing up a spray of dry snow. It was exhilarating and something totally new for the young man and he savoured every moment. The dogs, as ever, loped above and around them, streaking through the snow.

He jumped down and opened the gates, four in all, and they arrived at the top and over the cattle grid. Jos expertly backed the trailer next to the stone gantry and they manhandled the heavy churns off it and loaded the waiting empties for the morning. This time there was no sign of the postman and, pulling Beelzebub round in a steep turn, they headed back down the lane.

Jos stopped by the second gate where, in the lee of the wall, the wind had swept the snow away as if with a giant broom. On the other side, the holly tree stood starkly at an impossible angle from the frozen ground, its shape planed and sculpted by the prevailing weather.

Holly trees are as mysterious in their habits as mushrooms. One year they are groaning with berries, the next there are none. Just as a field yielding mushrooms in abundance will stay bare of the fungi for no apparent reason for years. But Jos could always rely on this tree. Leaving Beelzebub to rumble away to itself and, with his nephew looking on, he balanced precariously on the wall top and drew a pair of secateurs from his Barbour. He snipped away diligently, the green twigs laden with berries dropping down so that he quickly had all the holly he needed. Scrambling down again they dropped the twigs into a sack, and slipped Beelzebub into gear.

It was an unforgettable day. Having put the holly in the toolshed, they loaded two bales of hay on to the trailer and set out to the rack in the middle of the five-acre field where the sheep were wintered. Impervious to the cold in their fleeces, they clustered around the tractor on the trampled snow, casting wary glances at the dogs while the men unloaded the bales into the frame, cutting the twine and spreading the sweet smelling hay along the troughs.

Before they were aware of it, the morning had slipped away and they found themselves sitting once again at the table, this time with a bowl of soup and large crumbly slices of Wensleydale cheese and bread. Emily's chair by the fire was still empty.

Jos looked across to Laura, catching her expression of concern and lifted his eyes to the ceiling. The glance was not wasted on the young man.

'She was out like a light when last I went up,' said Laura, as she spread a cloth on the tray, adding a bowl of light broth and cutlery and carried it upstairs.

Nothing was said around the table and the ceiling creaked with footfalls above their heads. There were muttered far-off words, then more footsteps down the stairs. The sneck lifted and

Laura reappeared, her homely face a study in concern. It was clear from the uncertainty in her eyes that all was not well. Jos got up from the table and she spoke quietly to him before he went upstairs. When he returned his face was grave. 'I think yesterday was a bit too much,' he said. 'We'd 'appen best get t'doctor to have a look at 'er.'

Only an hour earlier they had been gathering holly, just another little step to making it all a bit more like Christmas, and now the grey pall of worry was down upon them again, like rain clouds on Whernside. Walter was despatched to get Dr Norton, as there was no way he could be reached on a dead phone, and Jos took his subdued leave and went upstairs to sit with his wife.

The young man looked up to the ceiling again and there was something in his stance that stopped Laura in mid pudding mix, the broken eggshells and wooden spoon momentarily forgotten. It was almost as if he were watching or waiting for something, and in a strange way it was quite unnerving.

'I think I'll take a walk,' he said quietly,

reaching for the old coat and muffler. The door closed behind him.

He was quite alone, a dark figure in the bleak winter landscape, striding along the narrow path that led upwards along the side of the Ghyll towards the snowy heights of the fells beyond. At one point he turned and gazed steadfastly down the valley towards Keld Farm, the grey eyes unblinking and seemingly bottomless in their compassion.

Chapter 6

TUESDAY, 24 DECEMBER.
LATER THAT SAME DAY

WALTER'S LITTLE green van, heard long before it was seen, pulled into the yard with snow spraying from the snowchains. Jos was waiting for him, standing in his shirtsleeves, oblivious to the cold outside the porch door.

His question died on his lips, unspoken, as a four-wheel drive pulled in behind Walter. Andrew Norton walked hurriedly across the yard, black bag in one hand, the other outstretched to meet Jos in greeting. They had known each other for many years, and Arnold Robertshaw and Jeremy, Andrew's son, were still the best of friends.

'Not so good, I gather, Jos.' The two men

walked inside. 'Let's be having a look at her then.'

Walter crossed the yard, a puzzled frown on his face. It would be all right now, he thought, with the countryman's implicit trust in doctors. You would just about be shaking hands with the Grim Reaper before you "troubled the doc," but once done the confidence was total. It was something else that had caught his eye on the way back down the lane.

He had left all the gates open for Andrew Norton driving behind him and was just swinging the last one back on its hinges when he chanced to look upwards along the skyline above the Ghyll. It could have been a trick of the light but it seemed for an instance that he saw a tall figure standing motionless at the very point where the skyline met the snow-tinged blaze of the afternoon sun. He blinked and looked again and thought that he must have been imagining things, for there was no sign of anyone.

***

'Usual thing, Jos.' Andrew Norton snapped the handles of the black leather bag shut. 'Lots of rest and, hard to say it at this time of year, but not too much excitement. If she feels like getting up, bring her down by all means, for too much time in bed, you know, and the spirit starts to weaken. Emily likes folks around her.'

'Thanks, Andrew. Can I get you something?' Jos waved his hand in the general direction of the bottles on the table.

'No, thank you all the same. Still got surgery and it wouldn't do looking down somebody's throat and knocking them out with whisky fumes.'

They both laughed, a moment born of long knowledge and respect for each other.

Andrew left a prescription form on the table. 'Best you go down for this, Jos, if she suddenly feels sick again then it should help.'

Both men walked to the door and out into the porch, leaving Laura getting Emily's chair ready.

Jos shifted his feet, rubbing his hands in his hair.

'Come on up an' see us over t'season,

Andrew, an' tell Jeremy that our Arnold will be here, An',' he paused, and the doctor could see the wetness in his eyes, 'I know there's nowt tha' can really do, but thanks all t'same. A very merry Christmas to you.'

The doctor gripped his hand and walked off to the car. His four wheel drive ate the gradient up the lane but looking back he could still make out the tall figure of Jos standing at the door. He had seen so much in a country practice, from death to measles but, if he lived to be a hundred, he would never be able to understand why so often it was that the worst villains somehow seemed to glide through a life of profligacy, unscathed, while the good people, through no apparent fault of their own, caught it in the neck. The Robertshaws, he mused, true salt-of-the-earth folk, consumed with a natural honesty and goodness that did not shout from the rooftops. And now Jos had to watch, helpless, as she slipped slowly away.

What made it even harder was that little fledgling glint of hope he sometimes observed behind Jos's eyes that maybe, just maybe, Andrew could do something, yet knowing in his heart of hearts, as he would with any farm animal, that the situation could only end in the oblivion of death. Was it not Jos who once told him that animals could teach humans a lot about the dignity of death? That they knew when their time had come and accepted it as part of the natural course?

Andrew Norton sighed and swung left onto the main road at the top of the lane.

***

Jos had gently carried Emily down to her chair by the fire. 'Now then, you just sit still and let Laura get on with things.'

He took the Land Rover keys from the peg by the door and was about to head out when Emily's voice stopped him. 'Where's nephew, Jos?'

He slapped his hand to his forehead. 'Lord, what's the matter with me? I keep forgettin' he's here. No sign of him.'

Laura put down the tea towel. 'He's a strange one for sure. Went out before the doctor came an' didn't say nothin' about where he was going.'

'I hope he's all right.' Jos went to the window. 'If he's gone up the Ghyll there's unfenced shafts up there, and... well I never, here he is. The wanderer returns.'

There was much stamping of feet outside and the young man peered around the door. He nodded and smiled at Emmy, 'Are you feeling any better?'

'A little tired, but better than I was. Andrew Norton has been and Jos is off to the village for a prescription.'

'Can I come?'

'Aye, lad. Get your boots on.'

Emily looked so tiny under her rug but at least it was good to see her back in the chair and Laura was about to put a chicken in to roast. Jos added that they would not be long and he would get stuck into the milking with Walter when he got back.

***

The Land Rover bounced and jolted up the lane. It was as if every rivet and stanchion was

83

Chris Simpson

designed with one purpose in mind, to shake up any occupant unlucky enough to be inside. By the time they got to the top of the lane he felt as if he had been through a stone crusher. They turned down towards the village.

The light was fading fast and the skies deepening to velvet above the stone rooftops.

Jos parked by the surgery and went inside for the medicine. Greetings were exchanged and inquiries as to how Emily was keeping, to which he muttered, 'bearin' up' then together they walked on up the side of the square, nodding to this person and exchanging greetings with another. Jos stopped outside a store with the legend, "Harkers", above the door. It appeared to sell just about everything.

'I'm just goin' in here a minute,' he said sheepishly. 'Must get summat for your Aunt for Christmas.'

'No, problem, I'll have a look around.'

Jos, not used to such things, took his time in the shop, chatting here and there after the way of country folk and picking up on the odd strand of gossip. After much deliberation he finally settled on a shawl of fine Kashmir, exquisitely worked.

He tucked his wrapped parcel under his arm, and bidding farewells and 'compliments of the season,' went off in search of his nephew.

***

By now night had enveloped the village. The Christmas tree lights flashed and sparkled and above Tomkinson's electrical shop a large star of Bethlehem winked on and off. Whenever Jos looked away, the star of Bethlehem was still there imprinted on his retina. The age-old sound of a carol came drifting across the frozen square, 'Once in Royal David's City...' He was drawn to the sound. Standing a little apart, his giftwrapped present securely clasped under one arm, he listened and looked this way and that for any sign of Ambrose. Then he spotted him, standing a little apart from the singers, framed in a shop doorway, listening. Odd for a minister, Jos thought, who should be used to such things. But he seemed to be in a deep rapture, oblivious to anything but the carol. Well, maybe in South Africa, it being hot an' all, they didn't set too much store by carols. Strange though. He nudged his way forward and slipped some coins into the tin.

'Thank you. Happy Christmas.'

He watched Jos and smiled, 'Is it time to go?'

'Aye, lad. We'd best be on our way. Walter will be on his own again.'

'What did you buy?' he asked, as they walked on back to the car.

Jos muttered, 'One of them fancy shawls.'

He pulled the Land Rover round in a tight circle, up towards the road and past the singers again. The young man turned to look at them, watching them disappear from sight.

'That was wonderful,' he said.

They turned in over the cattle grid and down the lane. Shutting the gates behind him, Jos noticed that a low bank of cloud was moving slowly up and across the stars behind the rising moon.

'Aye,' he said, as he eyed it carefully. 'T'wind's still in t'north and that means snow at some point. You have to keep an eye on it in case t'sheep get snowed in.'

Down at the farm there was so much that was already familiar, the wedge of light across the yard from the mistel door, the puttering of the milking machine, the rattle of chain as Tip and Bess came on out of their barrels, the glowing windows.

Jos parked the Land Rover by the log store and, after some deliberation, hid Emily's present in the toolshed with the holly. Together they went into the house, going through the familiar routine of stamping the snow off their boots.

It was as cosy and cheery as ever, with the smell of roasting chicken and potatoes spitting in the fat around the bird. Laura, who never seemed to stop working, was making sage and onion stuffing in one bowl and bread sauce in another. Emily was in her familiar place in the chair by the fire, the face more pinched and tired, but the eyes alert and alive.

Jos opened the bottle of pills and together with a glass of water, gave Emily her tablets. He then made himself a swift brew and offered a mug to his nephew, who, now aware of its consistency, respectfully declined.

'Ah, well,' Jos said, as he set down his mug. 'It's that time again.' And he went off to join Walter in the mistel.

Chapter 7

TUESDAY, 24 DECEMBER. EVENING

THE SKY had filled with cloud. The wind that had blown so fitfully and bitterly the few days since the last snow had lost none of its sting, but it shifted cadence now down to a low moan, the very anthem of desolation.

They had sat, heads bowed, around the table as he said Grace. There was an extraordinary power to his words and Emily, who stayed in her chair by the fire, felt as if something or someone beyond the circle of light and warmth had infused the space between them all with an age-old and timeless presence. She could imagine him in his little church in Bloemfontein, filling the hearts and minds of his people with goodness.

Yes, she thought to herself, he's more than just a chip off the old block.

'Are you feelin' any better, love?' Jos looked across at her.

'I do believe I am,' she lied splendidly.

God, how much he meant to her. The lean, rangey figure with the greying hair, the calloused hands that she had known in so many different ways in their time together. She found herself, as she did so often these days, thinking down the years, the twists and turns of the life road leading into the half-remembered landscape of the past. She recalled the awkward young man, almost shy, who came to court her, the great harvest moon sliding like a cheese above the heady scent of the hayfields. Chapel on Sundays and Jos, ill at ease and shuffling in his pew to offset the shoes that pinched his toes, and those insufferable collars.

Then there was all their work together. Bringing in the hay; planting out the garden and, half dead with weariness, wrapped in blankets on a pigging rail, helping the piglets into this world, stripping off the cowls and putting them behind the rail in case mother felt like eating her offspring, or as was sometimes the case, inadvertently rolling on them.

Then there was their own baby. Right up to the last minute she had been making butter, ironing and washing and bottling and then the breaking of the waters, the pains. Andrew Norton as unflappable as ever, and baby Arnold, born in the same bed upstairs in which he was conceived. The gatherings of old friends and family. All around this same scrubbed pine table.

Tired haymakers, with a hundred itchy things and seeds down the back of their sweat-soaked shirts, demolishing meat pies, sausage, cheese and potato pies, salad and apple crumble, washed down with cider or "lotion". The conversation, she recalled, was always very local, very funny and rich in scandal and farming lore. Their laughter shook the beams and on not a few occasions she recalled the tangible relief of being inside and the hay home as the rain lashed down on the cobbles of the yard outside.

Emily sighed. The conversation over at the

table was desultory, the odd problem to do with the farm that had cropped up during the day and, the most discussed topic of all, the changing weather.

It was time for Walter and Laura to head on back home.

'Well, tomorrow it's Christmas Day then,' Walter said, and stretched his sinewy arms behind his head. 'Best be goin' because it's goin' to snow for sure.'

Jos walked over to the phone, picked it up and listened for a moment. 'Still dead, and we're none the wiser as to what time Arnold is goin' to show up.'

Casual goodbyes were said and they took their places by the fire.

'Look!' The young man pointed to the window where, whirling like dust, the snowflakes began their dance across the windowpanes. 'Aye it's doin' it's best,' Jos observed it thoughtfully. 'Lord alone knows what's goin' to 'appen if t'phone stays off.'

He paused by the side of Emily's chair, adjusting the rug on her knees. The young man watched them intently.

She suddenly took Jos's hand between hers, stroking and kneading the long brown fingers and then pressing it to her face. She looked up into his eyes with tears brimming in her own and tried to speak. But no words came, and it was left to the unspoken message in her face to tell him just what he meant to her.

There was silence save for the occasional spit of the logs and the ticking of the clock, broken momentarily by soft sobbing from Emily where she and Jos clung one to another.

He gently let go of her. 'It's time for your medicine, love,' he said. Walking across to the dresser, he took the pills from a drawer. The pain came in again like waves on some rocky shore, savaging the frail form.

Then it was as if the young man made up his mind. He walked over to her, looking down into her eyes.

'God, help me!' Emily's face was contorted with the pain and the foulness of the medicine.

'He can, and He will.' Again, words carried quiet authority. 'Miracles do happen. You must believe.'

She looked up at him. 'Nay, lad, I think it's

a bit late for all that. Miracles is what you read in t'Bible an' that were long ago. I've seen that many folks in distress an' tried to hope for 'em, pray even, but something's definitely wrong somewhere for nowt ever comes of it.' She gasped as a sudden swathe of pain cut through her body.

He took her hands in his.

'Please believe me. All it takes is a little bit of faith and leave it to the Powers to do the rest.'

Jos broke in, agitated and upset that their little world was being challenged by a well-intentioned stranger, relative or not. 'It's all very well to say that, nephew, it's thy line of work, so to speak, but for us ordinary folk it's different.'

'But you and Emily have been to the little chapel to give thanks for this, or pay respects to that, for someone departed, weddings or whatever. Surely it all meant something for that is faith, not just a habit.'

'Aye, well, that's as maybe, but miracle things don't 'appen now for t'times 'ave changed that much. It were different then.'

It must be that vile tasting medicine, she thought to herself. He still held her hands, massaging them in his long fingers. It had seemed as if nothing could stop the encroaching waves of pain and yet, slowly, almost unnoticeably at first, she felt an electric tingling sensation of warmth, spreading gently, soothing as balm and moving in over the bands of pain, extinguishing them one by one. It was as if the very source of the pain were being stifled at its roots and denied its power source.

'That medicine's working at last,' she said, drowsily, as the soft warmth swept upwards and over her, drawing curtains of blessed darkness across her vision. The pain dwindled and died and in so doing her head sank forward and, save for the rise and fall of her breathing, all was still.

Jos could stand it no more.

'Nay, lad what's 'appened? Can't you see she's had enough?' He strode past his nephew and bent down to take her in his arms, as he had done every evening for so long now. Slipping his hold securely around her, he moved to the door.

The young man unsnecked the door, standing back as Jos swung his burden around a little to begin his ascent of the stone staircase. She lay silently in his arms. Jos's face was bleak with despair.

'God help us.'

The door swung behind him as he made his way upwards.

The young man stood motionless in the centre of the room, eyes following the sounds across the ceiling above, whilst outside the snow whirled softly over the landscape.

Chapter 8

WEDNESDAY, 25 DECEMBER.
CHRISTMAS DAY

IT SNOWED all night long, with the skies clearing just before dawn.

Walter had promised he would help with the milking, Christmas Day or not. He had made heavy weather of the lane, chains and all, through the freshly fallen snow. Opening a gate and pushing the snow back against the wall, he glanced upwards.

Way over on the skyline, the tall still figure was again looking down towards Keld House Farm.

Walter shaded his eyes against the glare and, though he could not be sure, for a moment it seemed as if the figure waved in slow farewell.

He blinked, rubbed his eyes, and when he looked again, the skyline was empty.

'Who in God's name was that?' he muttered to himself, and carried on down the lane to the farm.

***

Jos came slowly up to the swirling light from the depths of a deep and dreamless sleep. Deeply troubled at first, the mysterious anaesthetic of slumber had smoothed away the creases and sponged the troubles of the night from his mind.

Slowly a sound came cutting through his awakening consciousness, like the jagged edges of a knife scraping across metal. He struggled to gather his faculties and then he realised. It was the telephone's shrill ring that pierced his senses.

The telephone, back on again!

He jumped from his bed, pulling on the clothes discarded like fallen afterthoughts upon the bare planks of the floor and, in so doing, knocked the clock over, noting with horror that for the first time since he could ever remember, he had slept in.

He rushed along the landing, barely noticing that the guest bedroom door was open. He half registered an empty room, the bed still made.

Down the stairs in his stockinged feet he all but skidded to a halt by the dresser. He seized the phone, oblivious to an unusual noise above.

'Robertshaw.'

The phone line crackled with static but the voice was clear. 'Uncle Jos, is that you?' There was no mistaking the edge of a South African accent: 'It's me... your nephew, Ambrose... from Bloemfontein. Did you get my letter?'

Jos felt his mind spin. He sat down, running his hands through his hair. 'Who... who is this?'

There was desperation in the voice on the other end. 'Me, Uncle. I wrote to tell you there were some complications with the seminar and I would have to stay an extra day in London. I've tried to call you again and again but your line was out of order.'

Jos found his tongue at last: 'You wrote to me...?'

'Yes.'

Dumbfounded, he could only add, 'I never got it.'

'Well, Uncle, I took the precaution of coming up last night and I'm here in the Fleece at North Appleton, and I...'

The sneck went up on the door to the stairs.

'Jos, who's that? What's going on, Jos?'

She stood on the bottom step, hands twisting over and over, her eyes bright and filling with tears, her face showing no trace of the ravaging disease. Emily standing. Standing as she had not done in what was it... how many years?

'Uncle? Are you there? Uncle?'

The dropped phone swung back and forth on its cable, ignored as they stared speechlessly at each other.

***

Outside, the snow that had fallen long into the night now lay banked, deep and unblemished, across the yard. Of the visitor there was no trace. Not so much as a single footstep in the unbroken surface that Christmas morning.